The Toads and the Tadpoles

by

Gentleman Jim

(James Roberts)

Copyright James Roberts (Gentleman Jim) 2019

All rights reserved. No part of this publication may be used or reproduced, stored in or introduced into a database and/or retrieval system, or transmitted in any form or by means whatsoever, without the prior written permission of the copyright owner and the above.

This book is dedicated to all those who have ever been bullied, or have ever been a bully.

And to all those who have experienced a change in life, that lead to a change of heart.

1
It was a beautiful spring day at the pond.
Four young tadpoles were playing.

2
Hey, what are you?
I’m a toad.
Ha ha, what a silly name.

3
You really think so, huh? And what are you?
We're tadpoles! We're way better than you.

What are you toads doing here?

We’re watching you.

Why?

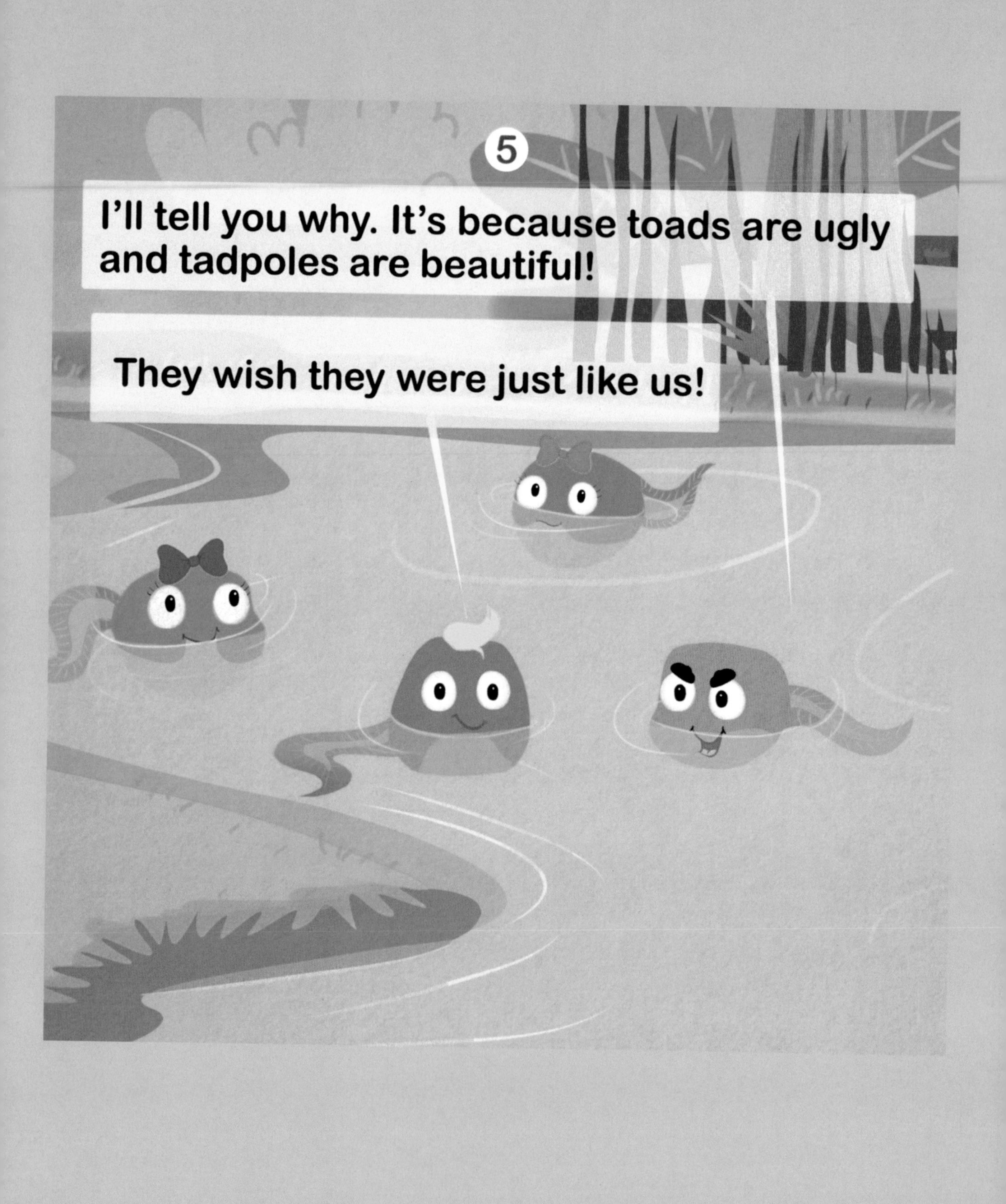
5
I'll tell you why. It's because toads are ugly and tadpoles are beautiful!
They wish they were just like us!

6
Let's go play
Yay!

7
What are you toads still doing here?
We're watching you.
Well, we're sick of that.
We don't want you toads watching us!
Why not?

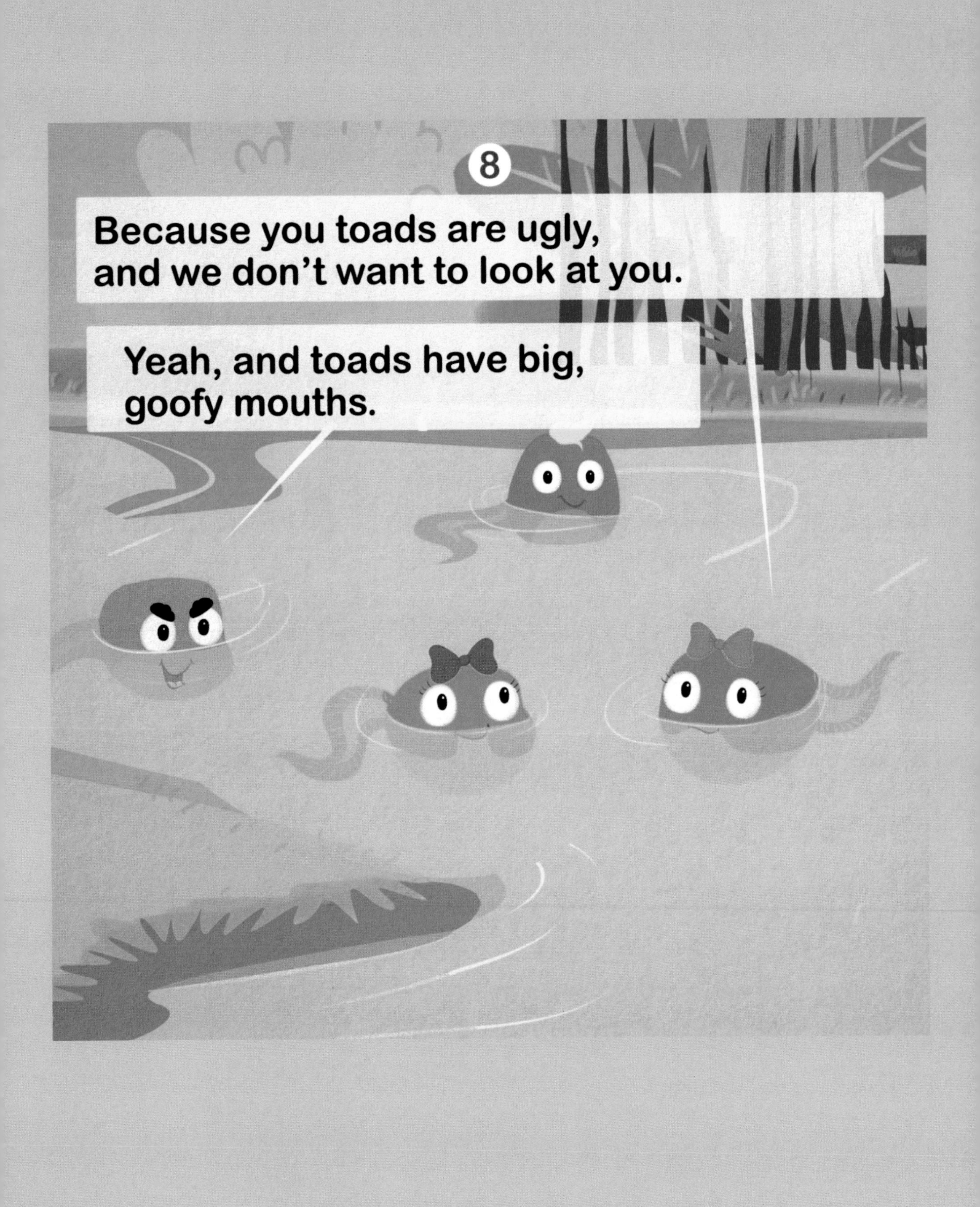
8
Because you toads are ugly,
and we don't want to look at you.
Yeah, and toads have big,
goofy mouths.

Look at us and our cute, little smiles.

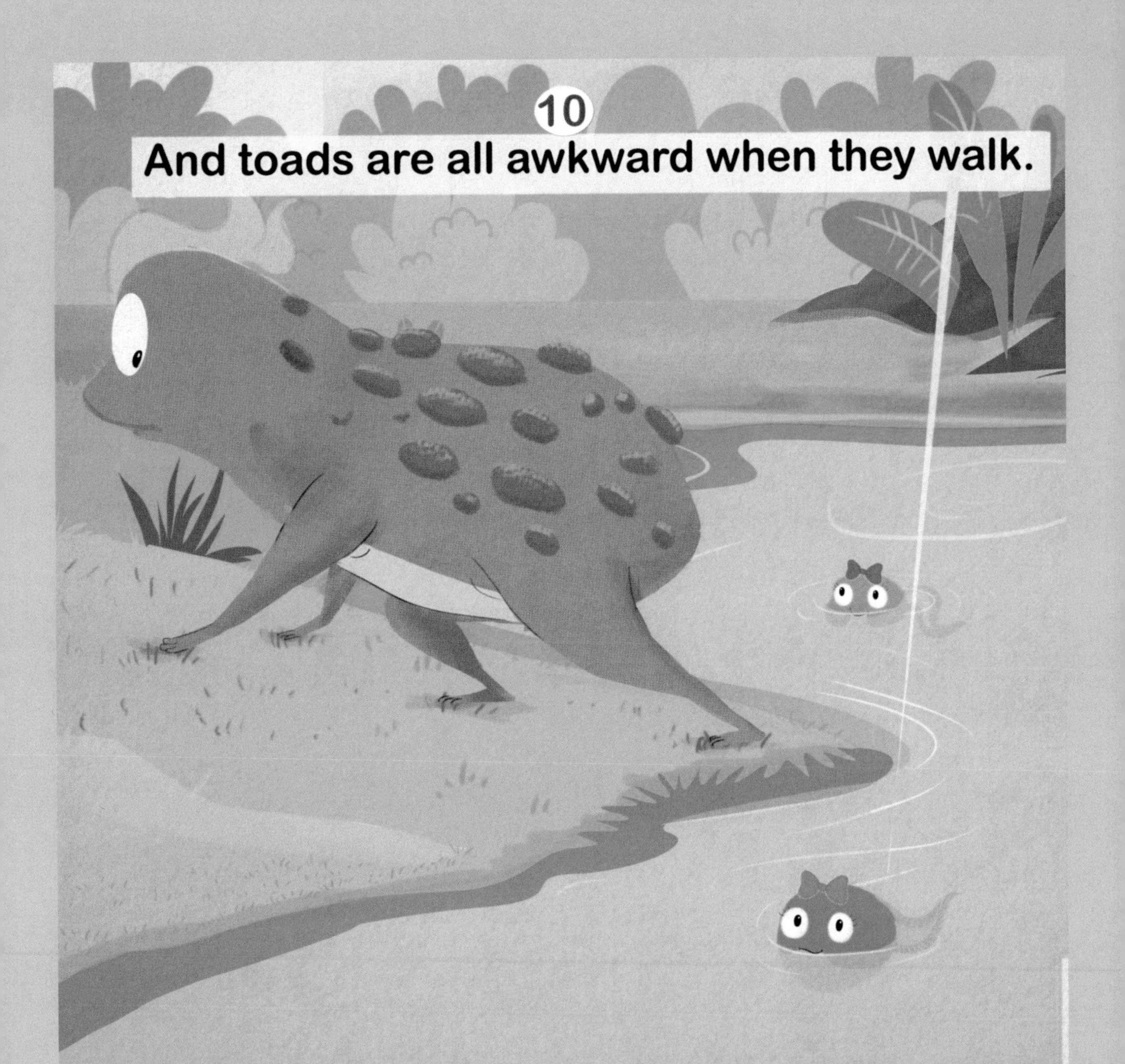
10
And toads are all awkward when they walk.

Look at how graceful we are when we swim.

Look at your skin too.
It's all lumpy and bumpy.

Not like us. We're all smooth and beautiful.

13
And your long, sticky tongue is gross.
You eat flies.
Yuck.

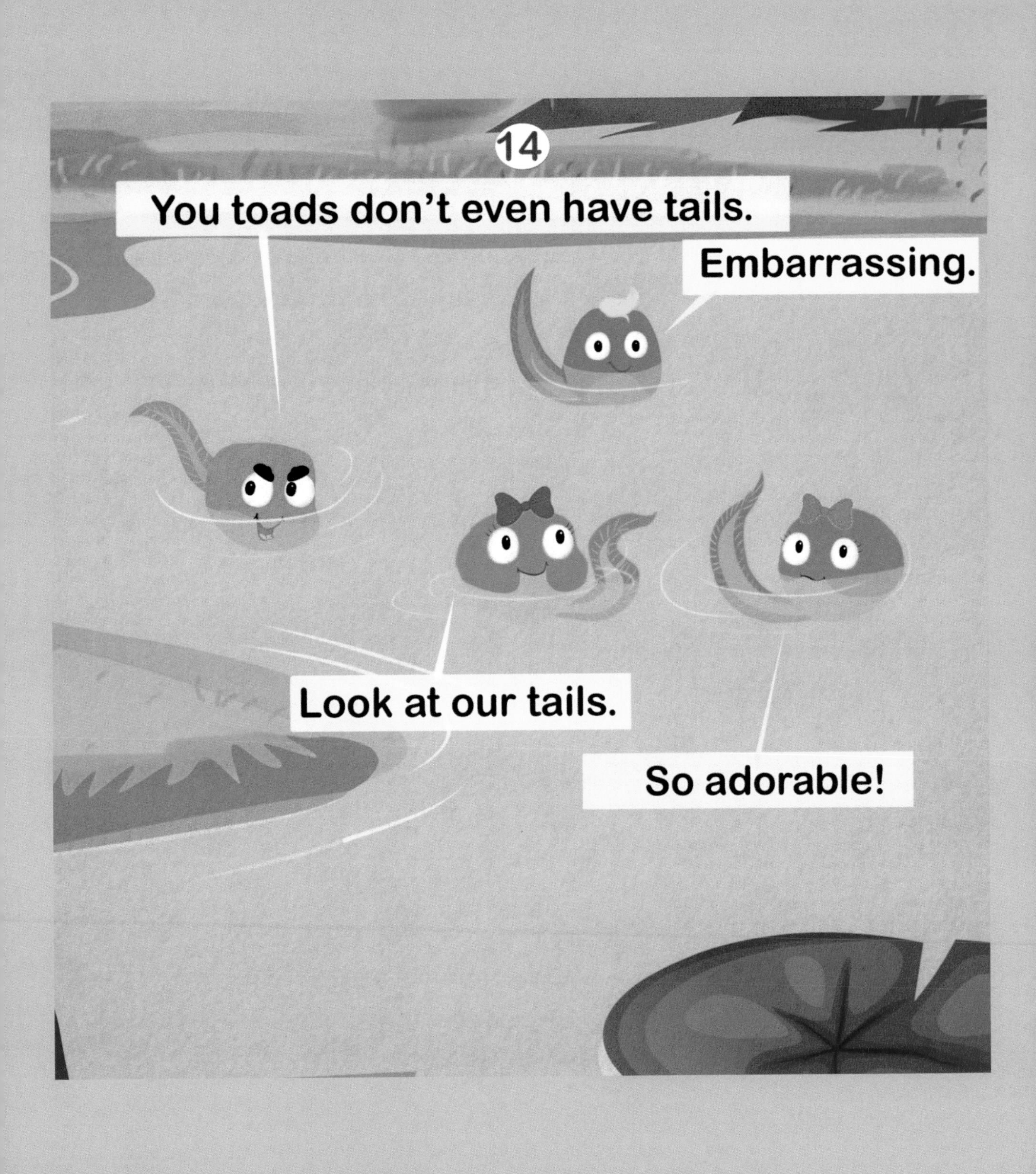
14
You toads don't even have tails.
Embarrassing.
Look at our tails.
So adorable!

Well, you tadpoles might be cute and all.
But it's not pretty to be mean to others.

16
You toads are just jealous of how good we look.

17
Ugh. Uh-oh.I don't feel so well.
What's the matter?
I have a big pain in my side.

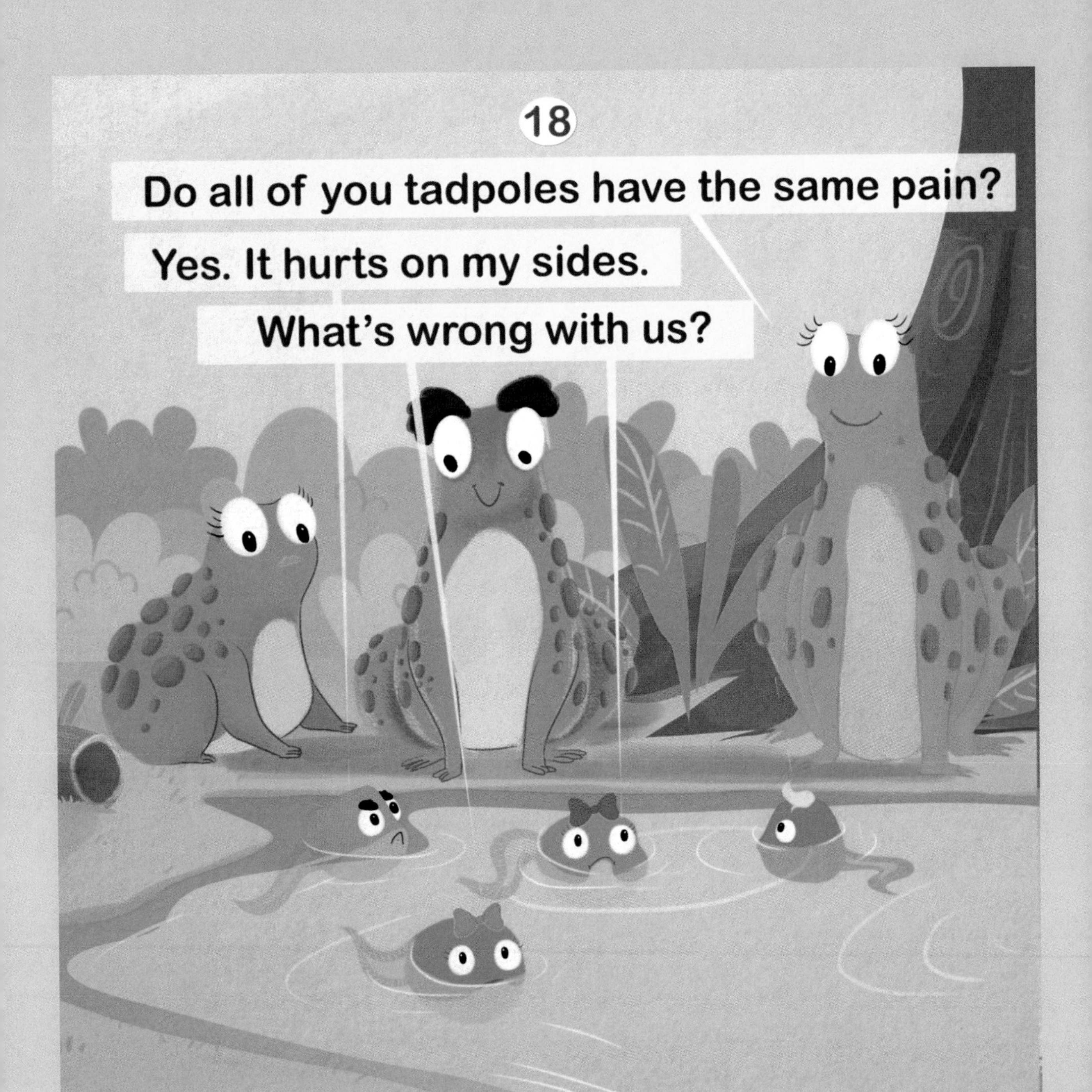
18
Do all of you tadpoles have the same pain?
Yes. It hurts on my sides.
What's wrong with us?

I think we'll find out soon.
Uh-oh. What's happening to me?
I'm sure you'll be just fine.
POP

What about my friends?
I’m sure they will be just fine too.
Uh-oh, not again!

Look at us!

Look at me!

Whats happening

22
Now my back hurts.
Mine too.
Now what?

23
I lost my tail.
Me too.
Our adorable tails!

24
What happened to us?
I don't know, but now I can walk.

Hey.
We all can walk.

What is going on here?
I wish someone could tell us.

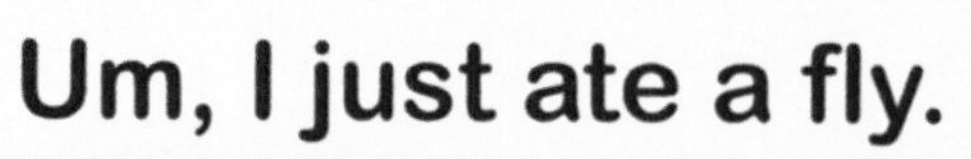
Um, I just ate a fly.

Excuse me, do you know what's going on?

You're growing up.

Growing up?

You mean, when we grow up, we become toads just like you?
Thats right

So you knew all along that we would become toads?

Of course we did.

Then why did you let us say all those mean things to you?

Yeah, we called you ugly.

And we said you have lumpy, bumpy skin.

And we said you walked all awkward.

And we said your tongues were sticky and gross.
I said yuck.

34

It's ok. We really didn't get too upset.
We were having too much fun watching you.

35
Yeah, why did you keep watching us anyway?

36
Because we're your parents!

37
Oh, now I feel awful about what I said.
I'm sorry mom and dad.
Me too. I'm so sorry.

38
Gosh, I’m really sorry too.
I’m sorry mom and dad.

Well, you’re all forgiven. Just remember this when you have tadpoles of your own.

So, are you going to make fun of toads anymore?

No way! We love being toads!

Well, that's much better.

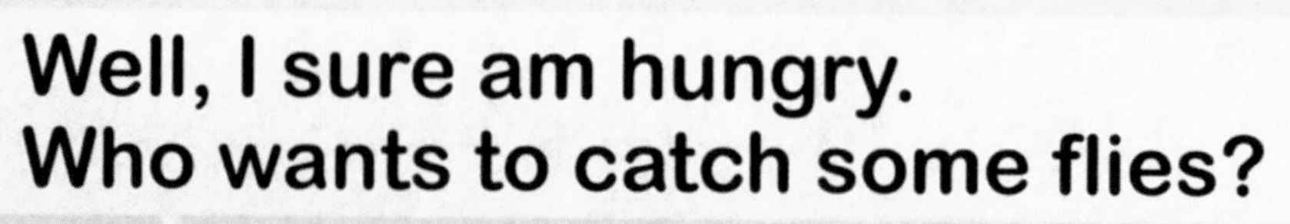
Well, I sure am hungry.
Who wants to catch some flies?

44
We do! Yay!!

If you enjoyed this book, help spread the word!

*Like our Facebook page: The Little Book About BIG Words

*Follow us on Instagram: authorgentlemanjim

*Visit our website: Authorgentlemanjim.com

Or consider taking a moment and writing a review for us at Amazon.com or Goodreads.com

Thank You!!

Other books by Gentleman Jim:

The Little Book About BIG Words #1-6

The Little Book About FUN Words #1-2

The Thrill Seekers

Gina and the Marines

The Little Book of Sayings

Special Thanks to:

Brenda Van Niekerk

For formatting this book

For publication.

(Brenda@triomarketers.com)

Made in the USA
Lexington, KY
13 December 2019